THIS WALKER BOOK BELONGS TO:

_____

_____

_____

_____

pulling

balancing

measuring

teaching

hiding

sliding

cooking

tasting

throwing

pointing

stretching

tickling

finding

hiding

climbing

standing

marching

waiting

For Alice

First published 1994 by Walker Books Ltd
87 Vauxhall Walk, London SE11 5HJ

This edition published 1995

4 6 8 10 9 7 5 3

This book has been typeset in Plantin.

Printed in Hong Kong

British Library Cataloguing in Publication Data
A catalogue record for this book is
available from the British Library.

ISBN 0-7445-3655-3

Hiding

Shirley Hughes

WALKER BOOKS

AND SUBSIDIARIES

LONDON • BOSTON • SYDNEY

You can't see me, I'm hiding!

Here I am.

I'm hiding again!
Bet you can't find me this time!

Under a bush in the garden
is a very good place to hide.

So is a big
umbrella,

or down at the end
of the bed.

Sometimes Dad hides behind a newspaper.

And Mum hides behind a book on the sofa.

You can even hide under a hat.

Tortoises hide inside their shells
when they aren't feeling friendly,

and hamsters hide right at the
back of their cages when they
want to go to sleep.

When the baby hides his eyes
he thinks you can't see him.
But he's there all the time!

A lot of things seem to hide –
the moon behind the clouds,

and the sun behind the trees.

Flowers need to hide in the ground
in wintertime.

But they come peeping out again
in the spring.

Buster always hides when it's time
for his bath,

and so does Mum's purse when we're
all ready to go out shopping.

Our favourite place to hide is behind the kitchen door. Then we jump out – BOO!

And can you guess
who's hiding behind
these curtains?

You're right!
Now we're coming out –
is everyone clapping?

pulling

balancing

measuring

teaching

hiding

sliding

cooking

tasting

throwing

pointing

stretching

tickling

finding

hiding

climbing

standing

marching

waiting

MORE WALKER PAPERBACKS
For You to Enjoy

Also by Shirley Hughes

BOUNCING / CHATTING / GIVING / HIDING

Each of the books in this series for pre-school children takes a single everyday verb and entertainingly shows some of its many meanings and applications.

"There's so much to look at, so much to read in Shirley Hughes' books." *Children's Books of the Year*

0-7445-3652-9 *Bouncing*
0-7445-3654-5 *Chatting*
0-7445-3653-7 *Giving*
0-7445-3655-3 *Hiding*
£4.50 each

OUT AND ABOUT

Eighteen richly-illustrated poems portray the weather and activities associated with the various seasons.

"Hughes at her best. Simple, evocative rhymes conjure up images that then explode in the magnificent richness of her paintings." *The Guardian*

0-7445-1422-3 £4.99

TALES FROM TROTTER STREET

"Shirley Hughes is one of the all-time greats and her new series accurately describes the life of contemporary city kids." *Susan Hill, Today*

0-7445-2012-6 *Wheels* £4.99
0-7445-2032-0 *Angel Mae* £4.99
0-7445-2357-5 *The Snow Lady* £4.99
0-7445-2033-9 *The Big Concrete Lorry* £4.99

Walker Paperbacks are available from most booksellers, or by post from B.B.C.S., P.O. Box 941, Hull, North Humberside HU1 3YQ
24 hour telephone credit card line 01482 224626

To order, send: Title, author, ISBN number and price for each book ordered, your full name and address, cheque or postal order payable to BBCS for the total amount and allow the following for postage and packing:
UK and BFPO: £1.00 for the first book, and 50p for each additional book to a maximum of £3.50.
Overseas and Eire: £2.00 for the first book, £1.00 for the second and 50p for each additional book.

Prices and availability are subject to change without notice.